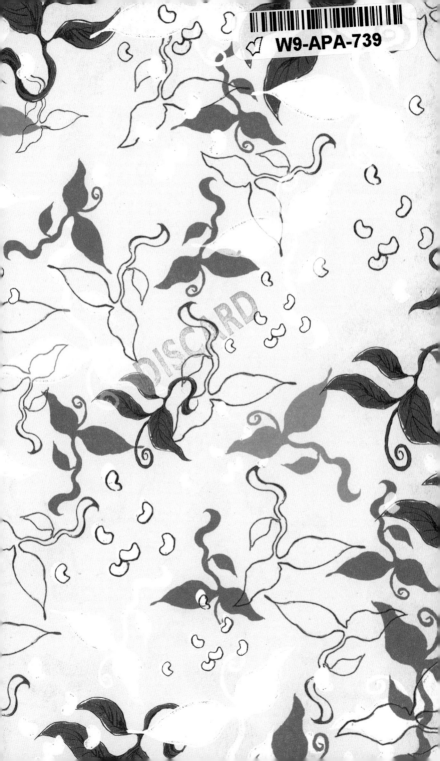

After HAPPILY —EVER— AFTER

The Three Little Pigs
Go Camping

After Happily Ever After is published by Stone Arch Books
A Capstone Imprint
1710 Roe Crest Drive
North Mankato, Minnesota 56003
www.capstonepub.com

First published by Orchard Books, a division of Hachette Children's Books
338 Euston Road, London NW1 3BH, United Kingdom

Library of Congress Cataloging-in-Publication Data is available
on the Library of Congress website.

ISBN-13: 978-1-4342 -7952-1 (hardcover)
ISBN-13: 978-1-4342-7958-3 (paperback)

Summary: The Three Little Pigs are going on a camping trip! The Third Little
Pig likes to plan everything, but always misses out on the fun. Perhaps his
brothers can help!

Designer: Russell Griesmer
Photo Credits: ShutterStock/Maaike Boot, 4, 5, 51

Printed in the United States of America in North Mankato, Minnesota.
032015   008805R

After HAPPILY -EVER- AFTER

The Three Little Pigs Go Camping

by TONY BRADMAN

illustrated by SARAH WARBURTON

 STONE ARCH BOOKS®

a capstone imprint

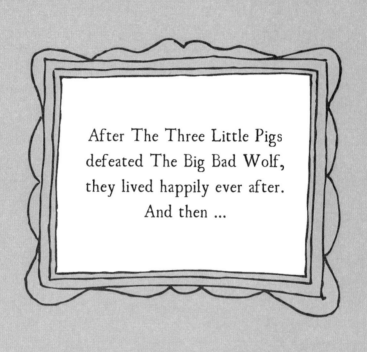

After The Three Little Pigs
defeated The Big Bad Wolf,
they lived happily ever after.
And then ...

The Third Little Pig looked at his list and smiled. He had finished all the tasks he had set for himself. The washing was done. The ironing was done.

The vacuuming, dusting, and scrubbing were all done as well.

This was definitely how he liked his life to be. His lovely brick house was nice and tidy, everything organized, sorted, and totally under control.

Now he could relax, and maybe even watch the new wildlife program he had read about.

But then again, maybe not. There was always so much that needed to be done! He should spend the evening thinking ahead and writing up lists of tasks for the next few weeks. Self-discipline was the secret to his successful life.

Suddenly his phone rang, almost making him jump out of his skin.

"Hey, big brother!" squeaked the voice on the line. "How are things?"

The Third Little Pig sighed. It was his middle brother, The Second Little Pig. There was a youngest brother as well, The First Little Pig.

The Third Little Pig could hear him
squeaking away too, so he knew his brothers
were together.

"I can't talk at the moment," said The
Third Little Pig. "I'm busy."

"Writing one of your to-do lists, I'll bet!" squealed The Second Little pig with a laugh.

"Well, I want you to cross out whatever the first item is and make it this — a camping trip with your brothers! Trust me, it's going to be fantastic!"

"Yeah, the best vacation you'll ever have!" squeaked The First Little Pig.

FOREST CAMPING
Deluxe

"I'm sorry, but I really don't think I can fit it in," said The Third Little Pig.

"Sure I can't tempt you?" said The Second Little Pig. "We've booked a place at Forest Camping Deluxe, so we're going whether you come with us or not."

The Third Little Pig frowned. He was very fond of his brothers, but they were utterly hopeless in all sorts of ways. In fact, quite often they were real trouble magnets.

Take that unpleasant episode with The Big Bad Wolf, for instance.

Anyone with half a brain would realize
that only a brick house could keep out such
a scary beast. But The First Little Pig had
quickly built his house of straw so he would
have more time for fun.

And The Second Little Pig had built his
house out of sticks, just to be different.

Then the huffing and puffing had started.

It didn't take long for both pigs to come running to The Third Little Pig. His brick house had kept the pigs safe.

Not that The First and Second Little Pigs had been terribly grateful. It hadn't been long before they'd moved out again, even though their parents had hired a friendly security guard to look after all of them.

And they would probably get into trouble on this camping trip, thought The Third Little Pig. So he didn't have much choice. He would have to go along to keep them out of trouble.

"All right then, count me in," he said with a sigh. "But I'll need to do some planning."

"Now there's a surprise," laughed The Second Little Pig. "You don't have a lot of time, though, big bro. We'll be round to pick you up in the morning!"

"WHAT?" squealed The Third Little Pig, horrified. "That's way too soon!"

That evening The Third Little Pig worked
hard packing, reading about the campsite,
and making notes and lists.

He slept badly, and almost hit the ceiling when his alarm clock woke him.

As always, his brothers were late and didn't arrive until well after lunch. The Third Little Pig was angry with them, but they weren't bothered.

They threw his luggage into their battered old van and roared off down the road.

"Wow, this is so great!" said The First
Little Pig when they reached the campsite.
"I think there's a river beyond those trees.
Let's check it out!"

"What about putting up the tent and
getting unpacked?" said The Third Little Pig.
"I can't possibly go anywhere until I'm all
settled in!"

"Oh, we can do all that stuff later," The First Little Pig said.

"Chill out, man," said The Second Little Pig. "You're on vacation."

"So?" said The Third Little Pig. "What difference does that make?"

"Oh well, suit yourself," said The First Little Pig. "See you later!"

The Third Little Pig watched his brothers scamper away.

A strange feeling passed through him, almost as if he were jealous of them.

But then his self-discipline kicked in. He gritted his teeth, and he got down to work.

It was quite dark by the time his brothers came back to the tent. They were laughing and talking, obviously excited.

The Third Little Pig opened his mouth to yell at them for being gone so long, but he never got the chance.

"You should have seen it, big brother!"
said The First Little Pig. "A whole herd of
deer came down to the river! And we saw a
couple of otters, too!"

"That wasn't the best thing though, was it?" said The Second Little Pig. "What about that eagle, then? I never thought I'd see one in the forest!"

The Third Little Pig definitely felt jealous now. They were so lucky to have seen such things! Thank goodness he had made plans to see some wonderful wildlife himself.

Although his plans didn't quite work out as he had hoped.

The next day he wanted to go to a wildlife sanctuary he had read about. It was the first item on his list, and he couldn't think of doing anything else.

The Second Little Pig, however, didn't seem all that excited.

"But it's really popular," said The Third Little Pig. "Everyone goes there!"

"Exactly," said The Second Little Pig. "I'd rather go somewhere different."

So The Third Little Pig went to the wildlife sanctuary on his own. It turned out to be a major disappointment, with lots of tourists and not many wild creatures.

And his brothers had much better luck
where they had gone.

"You'll never believe what we saw today!"
said The Second Little Pig.

The Third Little Pig listened unhappily
as his brothers revealed they had stumbled
onto a family of beavers that was building
a dam.

And they had seen even more amazing birds, and then there had been that herd of wild buffalo!

That evening, The Three Little Pigs sat around their campfire eating a tasty supper. Two of them were cheerful. But one was looking very gloomy indeed.

"Cheer up, big brother!" said The Second Little Pig. "Why the glum face?"

"Yeah, you seem to be having a really bad time," said The First Little Pig.

"I am, and I don't understand it!"
squealed The Third Little Pig. "How come I
keep missing out on seeing all this fantastic
wildlife? What am I doing wrong?"

"Maybe you do too much planning," said The First Little Pig. "Of course, it's good to think ahead, but sometimes you should just go with the flow."

"Or do something different," said The Second Little Pig. "It works for me."

It worked for The Third Little Pig as well.
The next morning, he got up and looked at
his list.

Then he took a deep breath, and let his
brothers decide what they were all going
to do.

And thanks to them, he saw some amazing things!

A few days later, his brothers took The Third Little Pig back to his lovely brick house.

He waved happily as they roared off in their battered old van and went inside.

Everything was just as he had left it, but there was work to be done.

The Third Little Pig couldn't help himself. He had to sit and write a list. But he added three extra items:

1. Go with the flow (occasionally).

2. Do something different (once in a while).

3. Be sure to have plenty of fun (always)!

So, much to his amazement, The Third Little Pig managed to live HAPPILY EVER AFTER!

THE END

ABOUT THE AUTHOR

Tony Bradman writes for children of all ages. He is particularly well known for his top-selling Dilly the Dinosaur series. His other titles include the Happily Ever After series, *The Orchard Book of Heroes and Villains*, and *The Orchard Book of Swords, Sorcerers*, and *Superheroes*. Tony lives in South East London.

ABOUT THE ILLUSTRATOR

Sarah Warburton is a rising star in children's books. She is the illustrator of the Rumblewick series, which has been very well received at an international level. The series spans across both picture books and fiction. She has also illustrated nonfiction titles and the Happily Ever After series. She lives in Bristol, England, with her young baby and husband.

GLOSSARY

battered (BAT-urd) — worn down

episode (EP-uh-sode) — an event

glum (GLUHM) — gloomy and miserable

grateful (GRAYT-fuhl) — to appreciate
something

sanctuary (SANGK-choo-er-ee) — a natural
area where birds or animals are protected

scamper (SKAM-pur) — to run lightly and
quickly

self-discipline (SELF-DISS-uh-plin) —
to regulate yourself for improvement

tempt (TEMPT) — to try and get a person
to do something you want to do

DISCUSSION QUESTIONS

1. Which of The Three Little Pigs do you relate to? Why?

2. The Third Little Pig was all about planning and being prepared. Do you think it's important to plan things or not? Explain your answer.

3. Did The Third Little Pig have the right to be jealous of his brothers? Why or why not?

WRITING PROMPTS

1. Do you think The Third Little Pig stayed true to his three new rules? Write a paragraph explaining your answer.

2. Pretend you are The Third Little Pig and plan another vacation for you and your brothers.

3. Make a list of three chores and three fun activities. After you do each item, write a sentence or two describing how you felt while doing the item listed.

THE FUN DOESN'T STOP HERE!